Keep Your Distance!

by Gail Herman
Illustrated by Jerry Smath

The Kane Press
New York

To my sisters Randi and Robin
—G.H.

To Catherine and Benjamin Fischberg
—J.S.

Book Design/Art Direction: Roberta Pressel

Library of Congress Cataloging-in-Publication Data

Herman, Gail, 1959-
    Keep your distance! / by Gail Herman ; illustrated by Jerry Smath.
      p.   cm. — (Math matters.)
    Summary: Jen learns about closeness and the measurement of
distance in inches, feet, yards, and miles when she has to share
a room with her little sister Lucy.
      ISBN 1-57565-107-6 (pbk. : alk. paper)
      [1. Length measurement—Fiction. 2. Sisters—Fiction.] I. Smath, Jerry, ill.
II. Title. III. Series.
PZ7.H4315 Ke 2001
[Fic]—dc21

2001 000851

10 9 8 7 6 5 4 3 2

First published in the United States of America in 2001 by The Kane Press.
Printed in Hong Kong.

MATH MATTERS is a registered trademark of The Kane Press.

I have a new baby sister named Sally. Sally smiles and laughs and kicks her legs. She is very cute.

I have another sister, too. Her name is Lucy. And Lucy is *not* very cute.

Now that Sally is here, Lucy and I share
a room. My room.

But Lucy thinks the room is hers.

Lucy messes up my bed.

She dresses her stuffed animals
in *my* clothes.

She sings the same song
over and over and over again.

And she's always right there—
one inch away from me!

1 inch

Before I go to sleep, I try to think of the good things about Lucy.

She laughs at my jokes.

She likes burping contests.

BURP
BURP
RP
BURP
RP

We have fun playing
shadow games and telling
scary stories.

Hey! Lucy's not so bad.

The next morning I try to get dressed.
It's not easy. I can't get to the closet.

I can't see in the mirror.

I can't open the dresser drawer.
She's always in my way. Every
time I turn around, there's Lucy.

I get a tape measure. I measure two feet. "If you can't stay on your side of the room," I say, "at least stay this far away from me. Don't come any closer!"

1 foot = **12** inches
2 feet = **24** inches

Lucy doesn't come closer, but she's mad.
She throws her stuff all over my side.
"Lucy," I say, "I can't share this room with
you. I'm moving in with Mom and Dad."

Their room is across the hall. It's farther away than two feet.

It's one yard away.

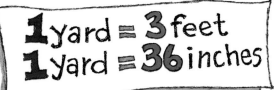

1 yard = 3 feet
1 yard = 36 inches

"Ha, ha!" says Lucy. "I'm coming with you, Jen. This is my house, too. So you can't stop me."

"Well then," I answer, "I'm moving to Jack's house."

Jack lives next door. That's farther away than Mom and Dad's room—six yards.

"I can walk there in one minute," I tell Lucy.

6yards=18feet

"Good," says Lucy. "While you're gone,
I'll read your favorite books!"

That Lucy! Jack's house isn't far enough
away from her!

"I'll move to Amy's," I say.

Amy lives 20 blocks away—almost a mile. I can ride my bike there in about 10 minutes.

1 mile = 5,280 feet

"That's fine, Jen," says Lucy. "I'll stay here and play all these CD's."

"Hey, some of those are mine!" I say.

Amy's house isn't far enough away, either.

"I'll move to Grandma's," I tell Lucy. Grandma lives in the next town. That's 10 miles away! But if I take the bus, I'll be there in half an hour.

10 miles = 52,800 feet

"See if I care!" says Lucy. "I'll just finish this triple-chocolate-fudge-ice cream all by myself!"

"Hey!" I shout. "That's half mine!"

I scoop out my share. So what if it's a little messy.

Even Grandma's house is too close. I'll have to move farther away—much farther!

But where should I go? I grab a map. "I'll move to the other side of the country!" I say. That's about 3,000 miles from here. No problem. I'll just take a plane!

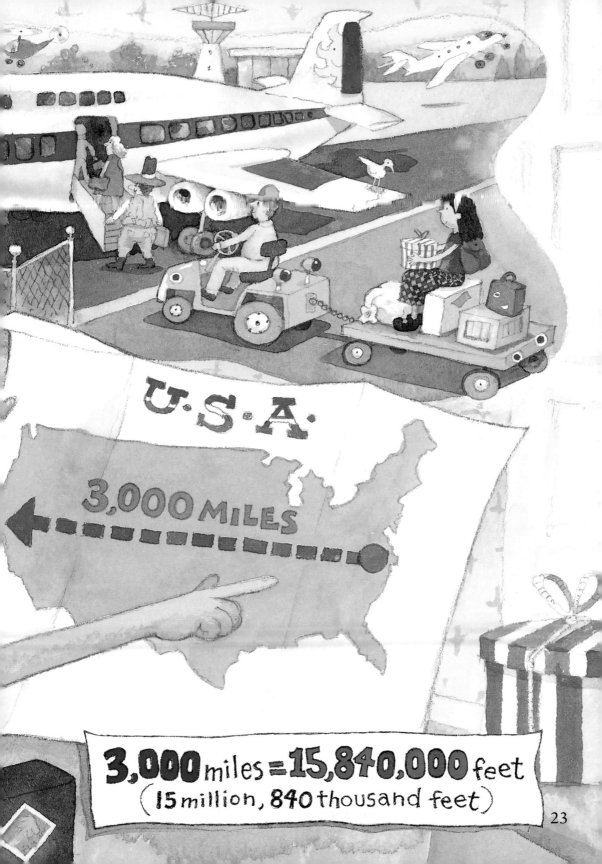

U.S.A.

← 3,000 MILES

3,000 miles = 15,840,000 feet
(15 million, 840 thousand feet)

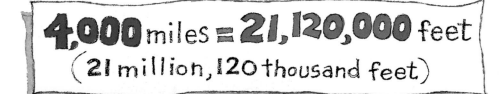

"Or maybe I'll go to a different country,"
I say. "I can take a boat across the ocean."
That's about 4,000 miles!

4,000 miles = **21,120,000** feet
(21 million, 120 thousand feet)

"Or maybe I'll go to a space school and take a rocket to the moon," I say. "I'll be 240,000 miles away!"

Earth
to
moon
by
Lotta Miles Togo

240,000 MILES

240,000 miles = **1,267,200,000** feet
(1 billion, 267 million, 200 thousand feet)

"You can't do all that!" Lucy shouts.
"Yes I can!" I shout back even louder.

Waah! Waah! Uh-oh.
Baby Sally is crying!

"Girls! Quiet down," says Mom. "You woke the baby."

She looks around the room. So do Lucy and I. What a mess!

"What's going on here?" asks Mom.

Lucy steps next to me. There is not one inch between us.

We look at each other. Then we smile.
"Nothing," Lucy says.

When it comes right down to it, Lucy
and I are very close.

I don't want to move anywhere. Not to
the moon, not to Grandma's, not even
across the street. After all, sisters have to
stick together!

DISTANCE CHART

How far can inches, feet, and yards take you?
Use addition patterns to help you find out.

FEET		INCHES
1 foot	→	12 inches
2 feet	→	24 inches
3 feet	→	36 inches

Add 12 inches for each new **foot**.

$12 + 12 = 24$

That's **1 yard**!

YARDS		FEET
1 yard	→	3 feet
2 yards	→	6 feet
3 yards	→	9 feet
4 yards	→	12 feet
5 yards	→	15 feet
6 yards	→	18 feet
⋮		⋮
1,760 yards	→	5,280 feet

Add **3 feet** for each new **yard**.

$3 + 3 = 6$

That's **1 mile**!

Inches, feet, and yards can take you miles!